Squeaky Cleaners

in a tip!

Vivian French

illustrated by

Anna Currey

Hodder
Children's
Books

a division of Hodder Headline plc

To Anna, with love and thanks
Vivian French

To Pamela
Anna Currey

Text copyright © Vivian French 1996
Illustration copyright © Anna Currey 1996

This edition published as a My First Read Alone in 1998
by Hodder Children's Books

First published in Great Britain in 1996
by Hodder Children's Books

10 9 8 7 6 5 4 3

ISBN 0 340 726644

Printed and bound in Great Britain by
The Devonshire Press Ltd, Torquay, Devon TQ2 7NX

Hodder Children's Books
a division of Hodder Headline plc
338 Euston Road
London NW1 3BH

One

Fred whistled loudly as he cleaned his
motorbike.

'Fred, dear,' said Gina. 'Could you be
a little quieter?'

'Sorry,'
said Fred.
He began
to sing.

Gina sighed, and went on sorting
out the contents of the van.

'Mops? Yes. Buckets? Yes. Brooms?
Yes.'

Nina came pattering up carrying the shopping. A large rabbit and several rabbit children hurried along behind her.

'I'm back!' said Nina. 'This is Mrs Rabbit. She says Sir Rattus Rat of Rattus Castle is in desperate need of the Squeaky Cleaners, and can we go at once?'

'Eek!' Gina looked anxious. 'Is that
safe, Nina dear? I mean – a rat!'

Mrs Rabbit hopped forward. 'Oh
quite safe,' she said. 'Sir Rattus is a
lovely rat – but so
forgetful!'

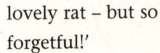

'Mother says his nasty rubbish blows into our nice tidy warren,' said a little rabbit. 'Mother says it sm–'

'Betty!' said Mrs Rabbit. 'Run away and play with your brothers!'

Fred watched Betty and her brothers skip away.

'Hmm,' he said, and leant against his motorbike. 'Are you sure that Sir Rattus Rat wants his castle cleaned?'

Mrs Rabbit
clapped her paws
together. 'Oh, yes!' she
said. 'He promises to tidy up and ties a
knot in his tail – but then he forgets!'

11

Fred twirled
his tail. 'Is Sir
Rattus rich?'

'No,' said Mrs Rabbit. 'He hasn't a
penny. Oh! Of course! I must pay you!'

She brought out a large purse and
tucked it into Fred's paw.

'There!' she said. 'Now, I must be
hurrying along!'

Mrs Rabbit scooped up Betty and her
brothers and hurried away along the
path.

Nina and Gina waved. Fred was busy
counting the money in the purse.

'Mouldy mousetraps!' he said.
'There's enough here to pay for a week's cleaning!'

'Maybe it's a huge castle,' said Nina.
'Come on. We'd better get going!'

15

Nina and Gina hopped into the van.

Fred climbed on to
his motorbike.

'All right,' he said, and sighed.
'Which way?'

There was a pause.

Nina began to laugh. 'Mrs Rabbit never told us!'

'Oh dearie dearie me!' said Gina.

Fred pulled on his helmet. 'Hunt the castle!' he shouted. 'Let's go!'

There was no castle. Fred roared
round and round in circles, and Nina
asked every passer-by, but no one knew
the way.

'Nina dear, I think we should go
home,' Gina said.

'Let's just go to the top of the hill,'
said Nina. 'We can see for miles from– '
Nina stopped. She and Gina and Fred
stared. Walking along the road towards
them was a rat. He was immensely old
and thin, and wearing a top hat.

'I think,' said Fred,
'we've found Sir
Rattus Rat!'

Two

Sir Rattus stopped as Nina and Gina
jumped out of the van. Fred scrambled
after them.

'Should we curtsey?' whispered Gina.

'Ssh!' said Nina.

'Good morning!' said Sir Rattus. 'Can I help you?'

'Well,' said Nina, 'we were hoping that we could help you. We're on our way to clean your castle!'

'How very kind,' said Sir Rattus. He thought for a moment. 'But I'm not at home.'

'We could give you a lift back,' said Fred.

Sir Rattus beamed.

Gina helped Sir Rattus into the van, and Fred climbed back on to his motorbike.

'Which way to Rattus Castle?' Nina asked as she started the engine.

Sir Rattus smiled happily. 'Do you know, I really can't remember? But I expect it's where it was this morning.'

'I think we'd better go to the top of the hill,' said Nina.

From the top of the hill Rattus Castle was easy to see. It was an enormous tumbledown heap of tins and bricks and stones with a tottering tower in the middle.

Rubbish was spilling out of every door and window. There were scraps of paper heaped in every hollow, and drifts of old leaves and scraps and string under the walls.

'There it is!' said Nina.

'That'll be a good day's work,' said
Gina, and her eyes shone. Fred looked
pale.

The Squeaky Cleaners arrived outside
the front door of Rattus Castle with a
flourish and a squeal of Fred's brakes.

Sir Rattus woke up with a start.

'Mercy me!' he said. 'I'm home! Do come in!'

Nina and Gina and Fred collected

their brooms and mops and buckets from the van and followed Sir Rattus into a vast and echoing hall. It wasn't

possible to see the floor; a sea of
scrumpled and grubby bits of paper
covered it.

'So sorry about the mess,' said Sir
Rattus. 'Never can work out where it
comes from. Now, can I get you some tea?

A biscuit? Don't eat them myself – can't bear sweet things – but there's a tin or two about.'

'Maybe later,' Nina said, looking round. 'Perhaps when we've cleaned the hall?'

'Of course,' said Sir Rattus. 'Just give me a call!' And he vanished through a door at the far end.

'Butter my beetles!' said Fred. 'Where do we start?'

Gina looked around. 'Fancy that,' she said. 'It's mostly paper. It's not really dirty.' And she picked up her broom and began to sweep.

Three

The Squeaky
Cleaners swept
and swept
until the hall
was clear. As
they finished,
Sir Rattus
appeared
with two
hot-water
bottles
and a
bowl
of
soup.

'Wonderful! Wonderful!' he said. 'Who's for lunch?'

Nina and Gina thanked him for the hot-water bottles. Sir Rattus absent-mindedly sipped the soup.

Fred picked up a handful of scraps of
paper and peered at them. 'I see you
enjoy reading comics, Sir Rattus,' he
said.

'Reading? Reading? Not me, dear boy. I lost my spectacles years ago!' Sir Rattus finished the soup with a slurp. 'Delicious! Now, what next?'

'I think we'll get on, if you don't mind,' said Nina.

'Mind?' said Sir Rattus. 'My pleasure! I'll go and prepare us a little supper. Back soon!'

'He'll probably bring us three old
socks and a Christmas pudding!' said
Fred as he watched Sir Rattus potter
away.

Nina grinned. 'Come on. We've a lot to do yet! Fred, can you bring those rubbish bags with you?'

'Yes,' said Fred, but he didn't move. He was reading another scrap of paper.

41

'Fred!'

'Excuse me,' Fred said, 'I've got an idea!' He whisked out of the hall and down a winding passage, carrying the bags with him.

Four

The passage was long and dark, and
wound in and out like the knot in Sir
Rattus's tail. On either side were crooked
doors leading to strange little store
rooms and odd little bedrooms.

Fred peeped into each one, and saw
bits and pieces and scraps of paper
everywhere.

'Hmm,' he said to himself.
'Interesting.' He picked up a handful
of scraps and inspected them.

'Sweetie papers, torn up comics,
bits of drawings . . . well well well.'

At the end of the passage was another door. Fred opened it and found himself in a larger bedroom with an open fireplace.

There was not so much rubbish as in the other rooms, but, as Fred tiptoed in, a chewing-gum wrapper floated down the chimney.

'This looks more like it!' Fred said to
himself. He sat down to wait.

Almost at once there was the sound
of squeaking and giggling. Fred's ears
twitched.

The noise grew louder.

Fred got quietly to his feet.

CRAAAASH!

Four little rabbits came bouncing out of the fireplace and rolled on the floor, laughing and squeaking and blowing chewing-gum bubbles as big as their heads.

'Aha!' said Fred. 'Hello, Betty!'

'Help!' said Betty, and she turned to dash back into the chimney.

'Just a minute!' said Fred, and the four little rabbits sat bolt upright, their whiskers trembling and their ears drooping.

'Please don't
tell Mother!'
said Betty.

'Please!' said the three little boy
rabbits.

'Please please please!' they all said
together.

Fred folded his paws. 'Why
shouldn't I?'

'She'd be so cross!' said Betty. 'She
doesn't allow us comics!'

'Or sweeties or chewing-gum or
biscuits!' said the second little rabbit.

'So we come here to play!' said the third.

'Mother thinks we're tidying our rooms,' whispered the littlest rabbit.

'I see,' said Fred. 'Well, you've been making a fair old mess!'

'What will you do with us, Mr
Mouse?' quavered the second rabbit.
Fred stroked his whiskers and thought
for a moment.

'I think,' he said, 'you'd better
begin by filling these rubbish
bags.' He looked as fierce
as he could.

'Yes. If you tidy up all these rooms I
might forget to mention that I saw you.'

'Oh, thank you! Thank you!' all the
rabbits squeaked together.

'Right!' said Fred. 'Now, I'm going to have a little snooze in this armchair. When I wake up I shall expect this room and all the other bedrooms to be spotless!'

'Yes, Mr Mouse!' squeaked the little rabbits, and they began hopping to and from collecting up the paper.

Fred sighed happily and closed his eyes.

Five

Nina and Gina finished the sitting-room
and the dining-room and the kitchen
and the bathroom. They went back to
the hall for a moment's rest.

'Phew!' said Nina. 'How much
more?'

Gina sighed. 'I'm rather afraid there
are a great many rooms down that
passage, Nina dear.'

'The one Fred went down?' asked
Nina. Gina nodded.

Nina sniffed. 'Humph. I don't
suppose it's any use hoping that Fred's
been busy.'

'Me? Not been busy?' Fred appeared at the entrance of the passageway, his eyes twinkling. 'Every room in this passage is spotless!' And he hauled out the rubbish bags, bulging full.

Nina and Gina were speechless.
'Dear Fred!' Gina said at last. 'How
hard you must have worked!'

Nina gave Fred a suspicious stare. 'Come on Fred – what have you been doing?'

'Me?' said Fred. 'Nothing! Nothing at all! Oh, there's something else I've tidied up. Sir Rattus won't have any more trouble with rubbish from now on!'

'But–' began Nina, and stopped.

Sir Rattus was staggering in from the kitchen carrying a large tray.

It was heaped with eggs and bacon and sausages and cheese and muffins . . . and an enormous steaming Christmas pudding.

'Wow!' said Nina and Fred.

'Goodness me!' said Gina.

'Breakfast!' said Sir Rattus Rat.